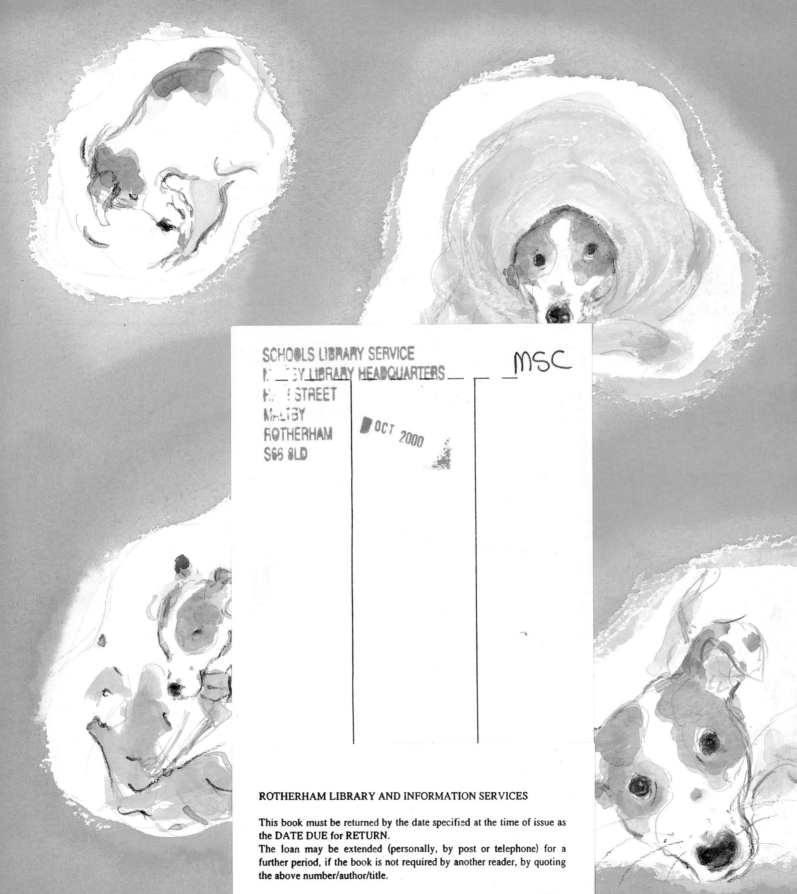

ORCHARD BOOKS
96 Leonard Street, London EC2A 4XD
Orchard Books Australia
14 Mars Road, Lane Cove, NSW 2066
ISBN 1 84121 247 4
First published in Great Britain in 2000
Text © Nicola Moon 2000
Illustrations © Carol Thompson 2000
The right of Nicola Moon to be identified as the author
and Carol Thompson as the illustrator of this work has been asserted by them
in accordance with the Copyright, Designs and Patents Act, 1988.
A CIP catalogue record for this book is available
from the British Library.
2 4 6 8 10 9 7 5 3 1
Printed in Dubai

My Most Favourite Thing

Nicola Moon ✳ Carol Thompson

ORCHARD BOOKS

rabbit's tail

rabbit

rabbit's ear

For Imogen
N.M.

For Basil
C.T.

Billy

Katie had a rabbit. A very old, battered rabbit
with one and a half ears and no tail,
but Katie loved him.

Everywhere Katie went, Rabbit went
too. Rabbit shared everything.

Mealtime. Playtime. Bathtime. And
especially hug-time.

"Rabbit is my most favourite thing
in all the world," said Katie.

mealtime

playtime

bathtime

hug-time

Katie knew that Grandpa's most favourite
thing in all the world was his dog, Billy.
Billy had floppy-down ears, a funny
stumpy tail and big soppy brown eyes.
Everywhere Grandpa went, Billy went too.

Grandpa had a big jar in the
kitchen full of special doggy treats.
Katie liked to watch Billy wag
his stumpy tail and look up at
Grandpa with his big soppy eyes,
until Grandpa just had to give him a treat.
In the evenings Grandpa liked to watch
television with Billy curled
up on the sofa
beside him.

One Saturday Katie and Rabbit went to Grandpa's house.

But Billy didn't jump up when he saw Katie. He didn't even wag his stumpy tail. He just looked up at her with sad brown eyes.

"What's wrong with him?" said Katie.

"Poor Billy isn't well," said Grandpa. "I think we'd better take him to the vet."

Katie hugged Rabbit very tightly while they sat in the vet's waiting room. Then it was their turn and Grandpa took Billy in to see the vet.

When Grandpa came out, he was alone. "Billy has to stay here," he said. "There's something wrong in Billy's tummy and he has to have an operation."

"Will it make Billy better?" Katie asked.

"I hope so," said Grandpa.

Grandpa's house felt empty without Billy.

"Will Billy be all right on his own at the vet's?"
Katie asked.

"Yes," said Grandpa. "There are other animals there
and kind people to look after him."

Katie knew that Grandpa and Billy were always together.
Billy was Grandpa's most favourite thing in all the world.
And now Billy was ill and Grandpa was all alone.

When it was time for Katie to go home, she picked up Rabbit and squeezed him tight.

Then she pushed him into Grandpa's hand. "Rabbit wants to stay with you, Grandpa," she said. "So you won't be lonely in the night."

Then Grandpa hugged Katie and hugged Rabbit all at the same time.

That night in bed Katie felt very strange without Rabbit.

She had Teddy instead. But Teddy didn't feel like Rabbit and he didn't smell like Rabbit.

Rabbit was far away, tucked up in bed with Grandpa.

But Rabbit would look after Grandpa,
and Grandpa would look after Rabbit. . .
until Billy was better.

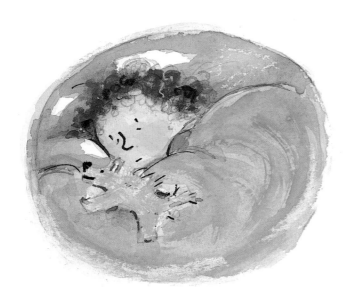

Rabbit stayed with Grandpa the next night too.
This time Katie took Fluffy Dog to bed with
her. But Fluffy Dog wasn't the right shape to
cuddle and his fur made her nose itchy. It took
Katie a long time to go to sleep.

The next day the phone rang.

"That was Grandpa," said Mum.

"It's Billy! Is Billy better?" said Katie.

Billy *was* better!

They rushed round to Grandpa's to see him. Katie gave Billy a big hug, and Billy wagged his funny stumpy tail.

"Here's someone else to see you," said Grandpa.
"Rabbit wants to come home now."
   Katie hugged Rabbit. "Rabbit is my most
favourite thing in all the world!" said Katie.
"And Billy's my most
favourite dog!"

"And here's my most favourite person in all the world," said Grandpa, picking up Katie and swinging her high in the air.

"And Rabbit," said Katie.

"And Rabbit, of course," said Grandpa.

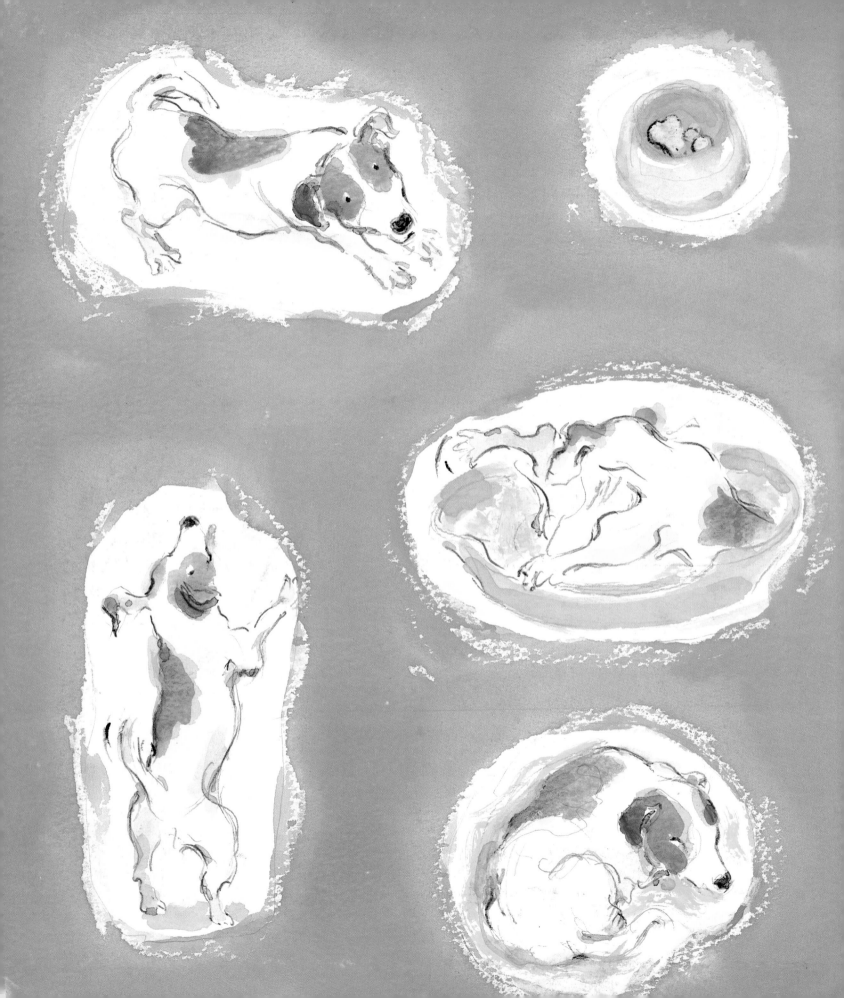